Grizzly Gas plc
Gas Towers
GAS 123

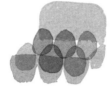

TEA

HAIRY

atishoos

FUR
wipes

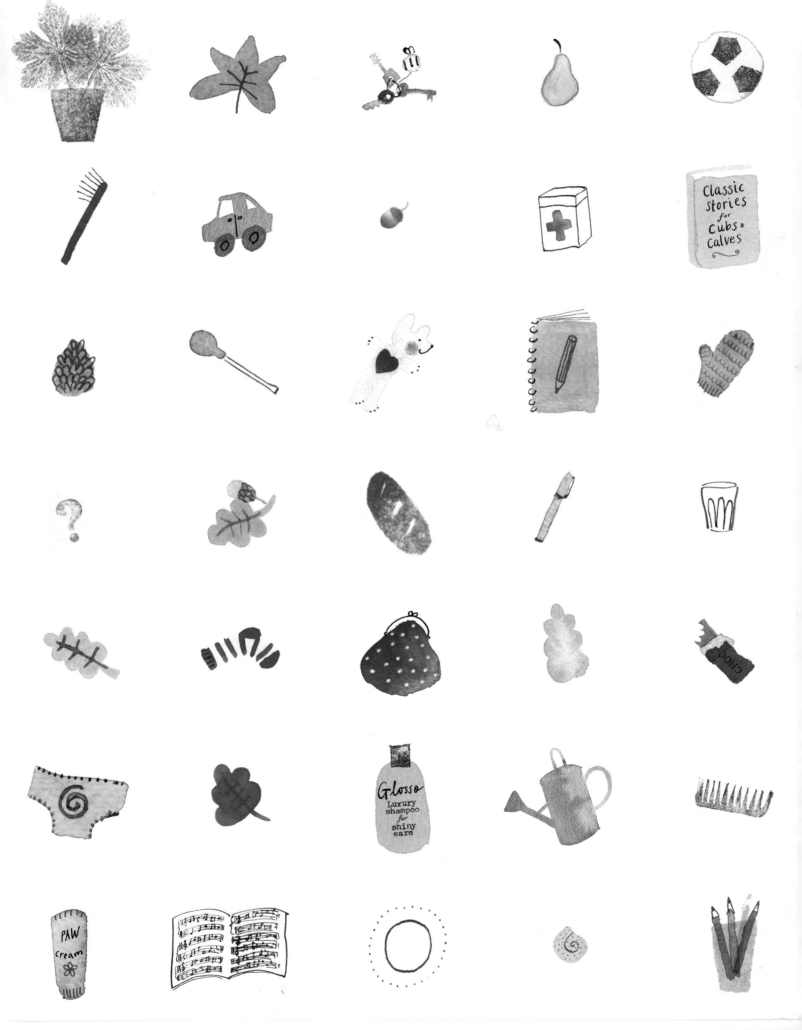

My mum is the strongest mum in the world.

WAHAY!

She's always been good at carrying things.
Which is great because I've always
been good at finding things!

Mum, can you carry this?

Can you carry this?

Can you carry these?

Come on.
Pop them in my bag.

There's always room for my treasures in Mum's bag.

Mum's bag
(aerial view)

Mum got good at carrying bigger and bigger things.

It wasn't that I didn't like my bike. I just got tired sometimes.

Café l'Ours
Café l'Ours

fifi's fur & Beauty

KNEADS BREAD

Jones & Cubs Ltd.

BEARGER BAR

KNEADS BREAD

Nearly home.

REALLY tired.

My mum never got tired.

Mum was great at helping her friends, too.

Can you carry this?

Sure! Pop it on the handlebar.

She carried Zebra's shopping,

Lion's laundry,

and Elephant's carpet.

Soon EVERYONE knew I had the strongest mum in the world.

She carried the lot. She even carried ...

WOW.

Mum probably had
enough to carry.

But it's not often you
find treasure THIS good.

Mum! Mum!
It's a triple header!

clatter

rattle

FUR wipes

HAIRY

VEG

splish

Recipes

ting ting

yoga

CLINK

CLUNK

It was just one thing too many. My mum began to teeter and totter and wibble and wobble, until . . .

Are you ok?

My mum wasn't feeling very strong any more.

Don't worry Mum,
they're only things.

Mum's friends rushed to lend a hand.

Lion phoned a friend
who could fix pianos,

and Zebra
mended the bike.

Flamingo made a lovely soup
with all the broken veg,

while Elephant tidied up.

And I picked up the
treasure for Mum.

Everyone agreed she
deserved a good rest . . .

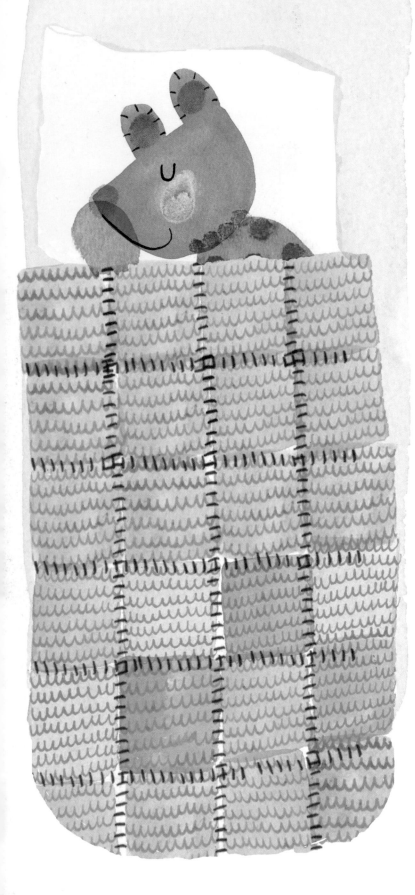

. . . and a bit more help.

How to
STOP cats
scratching
furniture

It wasn't long before Mum
began to feel right as rain . . .

. . . and ready to get
going again.

Honey
BUBBLES

Tra la la

Quack quack

Glosso
Luxury
shampoo
for
shiny
ears

Purse, check.
Phone, check.
Keys, check.
RIGHT!

But first I wanted to give her some treasure of her own.

This is beautiful!

I made it just for you!

WAHAY!

My mum is the strongest mum in the world . . .

. . . and I'm getting super-strong too.

ELEPHANT'S CARPETS

THE FLICKS

Let's carry this together.

Grizzly Gas plc
Gas Towers
GAS 123

TEA

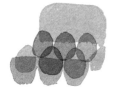

HAIRY

atishoos

FUR
wipes

Classic stories for Cubs & Calves

Glosso Luxury shampoo for shiny ears

PAW cream